Our Family Scrapbook

Inspirational Ideas for Preserving Favorite Photos and Treasured Keepsakes

Our Family Scrapbook

Inspirational Ideas for Preserving Favorite Photos and Treasured Keepsakes

PAULA WOODS

The Reader's Digest Association, Inc.
Pleasantville, New York/Montreal

A Reader's Digest book

This edition published by The Reader's Digest Association
by arrangement with
THE IVY PRESS LIMITED
The Old Candlemakers
West Street, Lewes
East Sussex, BN7 2NZ, U.K.

© The Ivy Press Limited, 2003

For Ivy Press
Creative Director Peter Bridgewater
Publisher Sophie Collins
Editorial Director Steve Luck
Senior Project Editor Rebecca Saraceno
Design Manager Tony Seddon
Designer Clare Barber
Mac Design Adam Elliott
Craft Design Emma Frith

For Reader's Digest
U.S. Project Editor Susan Randol
Canadian Project Editor Pamela Johnson
Australian Project Editor Annette Carter
Executive Editor, Trade Publishing Dolores York
Designer George McKeon
Director, Trade Publishing Christopher T. Reggio
Vice President & Publisher, Trade Publishing Harold Clarke

ISBN 0-7621-0448-1

Thanks to picture agencies for the use of images: Corbis, pp. 30–31, 33, 40–41, Getty, pp. 33,
38–39, Hulton Getty, pp. 42–43; and to David Barnes for his images on p. 33 (www.davidbarnesphotography.com);
Ray Goodwin for the images on pp. 34–35; and Earl Earl from Langley Scouting (www.langley.scouting.ca)
for the images on pp. 56–57.

Address any comments about *Our Family Scrapbook* to:
The Reader's Digest Association, Inc.
Adult Trade Publishing
Reader's Digest Road
Pleasantville, NY 10570-7000

For more Reader's Digest products and information,
visit our website:
www.rd.com (in the United States)
www.readersdigest.ca (in Canada)
www.readersdigest.com.au (in Australia)

Printed by Hung Hing Offset Printing Co. Ltd., China

1 3 5 7 9 10 8 6 4 2

contents

introduction

In today's fast-moving world of digital imagery, numerous TV channels, and lives spent on the run, there is something intrinsically comforting and relaxing about settling down to leaf through the pages of a traditional family album—to shut out the world and suspend time, if only for an afternoon, as you relive those experiences and emotions that truly come to life only through the medium of the photographic image.

Creating a scrapbook to be proud of requires very little special equipment—just a little artistic know-how. With scissors, adhesive, a few decorative elements, and some imagination, you are ready to assemble your photographs and ephemera, both old and new, into a comprehensive and stylish scrapbook that will be a joy for the entire family.

To help you on your way, this book is packed with ideas, suggestions, and step-by-step projects that will enable you to organize and display your photographs alongside those treasured keepsakes. Split into three main sections—talking to the past, special events, and everyday life—the book is easy to follow and covers tips on layout, professional advice on cropping and grouping, creative design ideas for displaying mementos, and framing and mounting techniques. It includes suggestions for theming your pages around subjects such as biographies, family trees, celebrations, everyday life, and those all-important vacations. In addition, there is useful advice on preserving and

repairing prints and some valuable information on
using design tools from computer programs to
enhance your pictures and layout.

For those who are a little more adventurous and who are eager to experiment
artistically, there are also a number of ideas that will extend your boundaries
and encourage you to make some original design efforts of your own. Why not try
our quick and simple suggestion of making your own pop art from a favorite portrait,
or create a unique "before and after" story (as seen in the best glossy magazines), or
try tinting and coloring your own photographs for great one-of-a-kind effects?

Whether you choose to adopt most of the design suggestions
shown, experiment with just a few of them, or use them as a
springboard for your own imagination, this book aims to show
you how much enjoyment and satisfaction can be gleaned from
the hands-on process of committing your memories to paper.
It will give you the means and the confidence to turn a simple
family album into an engrossing and absorbing coffee-table
scrapbook unique to you and your family.

So dig out those photographs, collect the memorabilia
that you've been saving, pick up those scissors—and start
preserving some marvelous memories that will be enjoyed by
you, your children, and your children's children for years to come.

materials

All the items required for the design projects in this book are readily available, and you may already have most of them at home. For a truly professional finish, take the time to look for the correct tools and materials—they will make all the difference in the look of the finished scrapbook page.

ADHESIVES

For attaching fabric swatches, such as a piece of christening gown, or creating borders with ribbon, use a specialized fabric glue (available in craft stores and some hardware stores) to prevent staining or bleed-through on delicate materials. For mounting photos, use special tape that is removable and non-acidic.

BRUSHES

Artist's brushes come in a wide range of sizes; most of the projects in this book require a fairly fine brush. Get into the habit of washing brushes immediately after use, and gently reshape them before storing them in an empty jar, in an upright position with the bristles at the top end.

COMPUTERS

Nowadays, computers are used not just for storing images but for manipulating them as well. If you have access to a scanner, this will enable you to convert photographs into digital files. You can reduce or enlarge your picture on the screen to see how it will look, or try out different colors to suit your design.

CROPPERS

These frames can be bought from specialist camera shops, or you can make your own by cutting two large L-shapes from stiff card. They are used to form a rectangle of infinite size which, when placed over a print, can be moved to indicate how your image looks with certain objects or subjects included in the frame.

CUTTING IMPLEMENTS

Whether you choose scissors or a craft knife, both need to be extremely sharp, as blunt blades will drag along the cut line, creating a rough edge. Practice using a craft knife on a cutting board for the best results. For a decorative finish, try paper-edging scissors. They come in a variety of edged designs, ranging from softly undulating waves to crisp points.

HOUSEHOLD ADHESIVES

These standard adhesives are available in liquid or stick form. Make sure they are water-based—for example, PVA or paper adhesive—or they will seep through and damage the image.

PENS AND PAINTS

There is a huge variety of pens, paints, and crayons on the market, all of which can be found in any good stationery or art store. Look for:

- Metallic pens
- Wax crayons
- Glitter pens
- Colored chalks
- Felt-tip pens
- Acrylic paints

PHOTOGRAPH MOUNTS

These traditional small triangular corners come in a number of finishes, including plain colors, metallic, or delicately embossed designs. They slide over the corners of the photograph and are attached to the page by a self-adhesive backing.

ROLLERS

Never press items into position with your bare hands. Even if you think your fingers are pristine, they can leave little grease marks or tiny smudges of adhesive. Instead, use a dry clean roller, such as the type of small foam roller sold for applying gloss paint.

STEEL RULE

A tough steel rule should be employed when using a craft knife. This provides a good straight edge and a fine uninterrupted cut because, unlike wood or plastic, it cannot be cut into by the sharp blade.

STAMPS, STENCILS, AND STICKERS

Decorate your pages with different kinds of stamps and stickers. Vary your stamps with different colored inks and use the stickers from the sheet included in this pack to label your pictures and objects. Buy some oiled stencil card and cut out your own shapes, and then paint the patterns or letters onto the page (*see page 11*).

PHOTOCOPIER

Use a photocopier to copy your precious pictures and other flat ephemera like newspaper clippings.

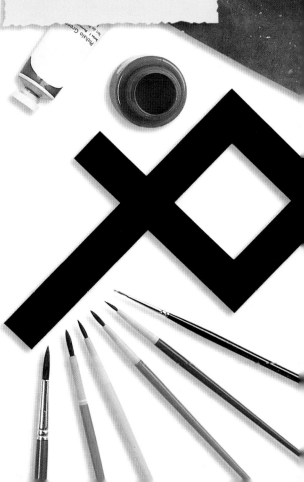

PAPERS AND CARDS

Look in any good stationery store and you will find a myriad of different papers and cards that can be used to add interesting design elements to your pages. Here are just a few to get your imagination going:

- Fine tissue papers. Try layering a number of colors to create some stunning effects.
- Handmade papers. Look for designs that incorporate textural threads, dried petals, or leaves.
- Colored foil sheets or foil-backed cards—or smoothed out foil candy wrappers for an inexpensive option.
- Rice papers.
- Plain papers and cards.
- Gift wrap.
- Paper doilies.
- Ready-made card mounts and frames.

methods

You'll use various techniques to compile your album but none requires any specialized skills. Here are some of the more basic methods, along with hints and tips for achieving a professional finish.

PHOTO MOUNTS

To position each corner mount accurately, follow these simple steps:

1 Place your photograph on the album page and lightly mark the point of each corner with soft pencil.

2 Remove the photograph and match the marked points to those on the tip of each triangular mount.

3 Once the mounts are fixed in your album, carefully tuck the corners of the photograph into each open edge.

CUTTING TECHNIQUES

The secret to a clean, even line is to cut in one continuous movement, without moving your blade from the paper. If you do remove your blade it is almost impossible to re-insert it successfully and continue without creating a small nick in the finished outline. When cutting curves, you'll achieve a smoother arc if you rotate the paper rather than the blade.

CREATING A SIMPLE FRAME

The easiest way to create a frame is to use your chosen photograph as a temporary template. Also use this technique to create individual backing mounts (without the frame overhang) by omitting Step 2.

1 Place your photograph face down on the back of your chosen frame material and, using a rule, carefully draw around the outline. Place the rule on top of the photograph so that it overhangs the edge, rather than butting up to it (so that the print is protected from any damage). Then remove the photo.

2 As you want the frame to overlap the edges of your print, you will need to measure a little way in from the resulting outline. Mark at least two or three points along each edge to ensure an even border, then draw in the cut line using a rule.

3 Decide how wide you want your finished frame to be, then use this measurement to draw your outer cutting line (as for Step 2).

CREATING BORDERS

Sometimes you might not want to highlight your photos with a frame or backing mount. Instead, try individual lengths of ribbon, strips of decorative paper, or other trimmings. Again, use your photo as a template to mark the positioning line. In order to achieve a neat, professional finish, miter (cut at an angle) the corners of the border material where possible.

1 Decide on the width of the border strip, for example 1 inch (25mm), and cut each strip to size as follows: measure the length of each side of the photo and then add on twice the width of the strip (2 inches or 50mm).

2 Lay the strips in position around the edges of the photo (in this example the ends will overlap by 1 inch [25mm] at each corner).

3 Using a craft knife and rule, make a straight cut through the border at the overlapping ends from the inner corner to the outer corner, thus creating an angle of 45 degrees at each end of the strip.

4 Glue the border strips in place, matching up the miters neatly.

TRACING IMAGES

Embellishing your pages with images relevant to the topic looks good, but if you're not confident in your own artwork, why not produce creative motifs by tracing images? Probably the easiest way to transfer images from one surface to another is by using carbon paper, available in most stationery stores. If you don't want to outline the original print, photocopy it first.

1 Place the carbon face down on your paper and hold in position with a little masking tape.

2 Position your chosen image face up, on top of the carbon paper and fix it in position with tape.

3 Using a pencil, carefully trace over all outlines. Remove both layers, making sure that the carbon is lifted cleanly away so as not to smudge the transferred image below.

CUTTING TEMPLATES AND STENCILS

Mounts and frame shapes are great to use time and time again, but if you have a lot of prints of similar size, make a template to avoid repeating the process of measuring each one individually. Follow the steps for creating a frame or mount, cutting your template from a thick (more durable) piece of scrap card. You can also make templates for complex decorative motifs, stencils, images,

and lettering to add colorful designs within your scrapbook. Just follow these easy steps:

1 Trace your design motif or lettering onto card, simplifying any complex sections as you go. Remember that each cut-out area of the card must still be attached to the rest of the card. This means your cut-out design is still joined to the entire piece and when you pick up the card, the design is embedded inside.

2 Working on a cutting board, use a sharp craft knife to cut along all outlines. Remove the excess.

3 Place the stencil in position on your page and secure with a little masking tape. Dip the tip of a small brush in some paint and apply to all areas of your finished stencil, working from the outside edges inward.

4 Once dry, remove the stencil to reveal the finished motif.

SUCCESSFUL RUBBINGS

The technique used in brass rubbing is a good way to capture the surface of bulkier items, such as coins or small shells, which will not fit on the pages of your album. As your album pages are made from thick paper, it is easier to create the image on separate paper and then mount it.

1 For a clear rubbing, your object must not move, so fix it firmly to a

flat surface with a piece of plasticene. Your object must lie as flat as possible, without the plasticene showing through anywhere.

2 Place your paper over the item and secure with masking tape.

3 Using one hand to steady the paper, take a soft waxy crayon or piece of charcoal and rub firmly over the entire surface of your object to reveal the design.

ADDING MEMORABILIA

Keepsakes are an important part of any album and to mount them successfully they need to be as flat as possible. While many items, such as old, curled paper clippings, leaflets, and even photographs, simply require smoothing out, other items such as flowers and leaves may also need drying. Both these things can be achieved through pressing.

1 Select four or five heavy books. Open one and line both pages with several layers of paper towel or waxed (greaseproof) paper.

2 Place your keepsake in the center of the lined page and carefully close the book over it.

3 Pile the remaining heavy books on top and set aside for a few days for flattening, or if you're drying the object, leave it to press for three weeks or more.

putting a page together

When faced with your first blank page, simply getting started can seem like a daunting task. Begin by reading the ideas listed below and then take a little time to plan your layout and overall design. This will ensure that you create a precious collection of your unique moments and, just as important, that you enjoy doing so.

GETTING STARTED

Before you begin to think about layout, set aside a few hours to sort through your photographs. Forget about which images will go on which pages and simply decide which photographs you want to keep. This is an excellent activity for a rainy weekend or quiet evening. Ask the family to join in for some amusement, and place each picture in one of three piles—one for the "must haves," one for the "must go," and finally, one for the "maybes." As well as finding many images that are not of a high enough quality to be included, you may also be surprised by how many photographs you have that portray the same subject and scene.

CHOOSING A THEME

Having selected your images, one of the easiest ways of presenting them is by theme. This book suggests a range of different themes to bring cohesion to your album, but these are just ideas; don't feel limited by them. More often than not, a topic will spring to mind as you are sorting through your photos. You may have a number of pictures that concentrate on a single person, or a hobby that you have often photographed, or you may find that many of your images reflect your fascination with architecture or landscapes. You could even try grouping widely differing images together using a dramatic linking color, or present the many events taking place in a particular week or month. The list, in fact, is endless. The only limits are those of your imagination.

CREATING ARRANGEMENTS

The secret to any successful layout is experimentation. Take a look through magazines and illustrated books for some insight into layouts. Also, before committing yourself to a design, experiment by loosely arranging your photos in various ways. Try combining different sizes of prints, grouping various themes (like sports, vacation, or family), and creating collages to fit your required number of images on the page.

Consider whether the story tells itself through your pictorial arrangement or if you will need to add captions, which in turn will require their own space. How are you going to add interest to the page? Do you need to break up larger banks of images? Are a few lines of text enough, or will you need keepsakes to back up your narrative? Do you want to use a different text font in order to combine the decorative with the informative? Are there any design motifs or framing devices that can add impact to the overall layout?

All these kinds of questions will be answered during your trial run, and taking that extra time will pay dividends in the long run.

MOUNTING AND FRAMING

Although you can display a number of your photographs by simply fixing them directly on the page, presenting your images in framed and mounted formats not only adds dramatic impact but also helps to delineate a group or highlight a particularly special image.

Think about the materials you will use and whether they complement the images they are being used with: for instance, a pretty lace doily or handmade paper may well add to a wedding or christening image but will look out of place framing a

picture from a camping vacation. Take a look around your home for inspiration and try placing a number of photographs against various materials, such as a piece of gift wrap paper, colored card, or even aluminum foil, to see if they make good pairings. Think about layering thin pieces of paper on top of one another to create a subtle impression of depth, and vary the colors to draw in the eye. And finally, take inspiration from the image itself— look for a dominant color or an element within it that can be drawn out and used on the page to help bring your two-dimensional compositions to life.

USING COLOR

Never underestimate the power of color. Placing the elements of your page on a specific color can make all the difference to your design, whether in the form of an overall background color or a few well-placed frames, mounts, or decorative motifs. Of course, you can use generally accepted associations, such as white for a wedding or blue for the birth of a baby boy, to add weight to your story, but you can also use the principles of color theory to enhance your layout. In general, you will find that bold colors appear to advance on the page while paler colors recede,

and you can use these qualities to enhance the impact of your layout. While a delicately patterned background will be overpowered by strongly colored photographs, using it as a backdrop to a simple black-and-white image will create a striking contrast.

COMPOSING NARRATIVE

Whatever your subject, it comes to life faster if your album's reader is aware of the details and history surrounding the event, and this is most easily achieved in the form of a narrative.

Names and dates, a descriptive piece, a witty anecdote, or general feelings about the topic are all ways to convey more detail. (Writing in the present tense helps to draw the reader into a pro-active experience.) Ask those featured in the images to record their comments, such as: What was their favorite part of the day or vacation? What was the weather like? What kind of food did they eat? The more people you involve in creating this family scrapbook, the more it will be valued in the years to come.

marrying old with new

Looking at a picture of a long-gone family member can be fascinating. As the years peel away, you become aware of common features and gain a strong sense of who you are and where you have come from.

Discovering that you belong to a long line of relatives with some shared qualities is just as fascinating for the young as for the old. So make sure you set aside a few pages in your family scrapbook for comparing past family members to those of the current generation.

Combining old photographs with new on a single page can be something of a challenge. Modern, glossy, brightly colored prints can often overwhelm the delicate and faded sepia images of yesteryear. There are several ways you can get around the problem.

One of the most obvious techniques is to use black-and-white prints rather than color in order to play down the harsh contrasts and help create a more harmonious effect. Turning your color snapshots into monotone is a simple process, as black-and-white images can be easily printed from color negatives.

Alternatively, you could simply photocopy your favorite images. Don't worry if a few of them are not perfect reproductions; this sometimes echoes the grainy quality of some older prints to good effect. Also, mounting a group of photographs on the same paper or surrounding them with a hand-drawn decorative border will instantly unify the page, despite any inconsistencies in color.

COMPARE AND CONTRAST

Pairing images of subjects in similar settings highlights family likenesses and shared pleasures while diffusing color contrasts. Setting a faded childhood image of a mother or father enjoying a simple activity, such as walking on a beach, alongside a modern image of their own children

Using old and new images together on the page of your album can draw parallels between past and present— especially if you show an older version of the same place or activity.

enjoying this same activity a
generation later helps narrow the
age gap, while still leaving room for
shared laughter at the differences in
bathing suits and beach toys.

COLOR COORDINATING

Picking out a predominant color in
modern-day images and using it to
frame or mount an older black-and-
white image will offer a visual link
between the two. So if your grandson
is wearing a green pullover, frame an
old image with a matching green
color to complement it.

STITCHED MOUNTS

Unify the old with the new using
retro-style mounts fashioned from
parchment paper. Punch a row of
holes along all four sides of the mount,
then thread twine or yarn in and out
of the holes. Use running stitch or
whipstitch so the thread is passed up
through one hole, over the edge of
the paper, then up through the next.

*The technique of
compare and contrast
can be used with places
too. An old picture
placed near a modern
photograph of the same
area shows the passage
of time to stunning effect.*

FRAMING TECHNIQUES

To complement the delicate edges of old
photographs, use paper-edging scissors to cut
decorative, fluted borders on contemporary
prints. This works especially well on modern
prints with white edges around them.
Alternatively, if you do not want to tamper
with original prints, you could simply
mount each picture on a rectangle of
decoratively edged paper.

recreating old images

There is an enchanting quality to, and something intrinsically appealing about, old photographs. Their often formal staging, their delicate sepia—or sometimes hand-colored—tints, and their quaint backgrounds make them unique.

Dressing up in costume to mimic the past highlights similarities and differences. The formal old portrait of the young girl on the right used next to the modern black-and-white photo provides a touching connection.

While the previous pages looked at juxtaposing old and new for a compare-and-contrast effect, these two pages look at ways in which new images can be made to resemble charming vintage pictures.

A glorious technicolor photograph can look out of place when set amongst older monochrome images. One easy way to rectify this is to use a black-and-white photocopier and copy the color photograph onto good-quality matt or gloss paper, then trim to size and mount in place.

Look back over old albums for ideas on how to arrange and mount your photographs. Old albums usually contain formal family portraits since photography was a luxury, with people as the principal subject and backbone to a collection. Resurrecting old techniques, by using protective page covers made from fine tissue paper, paper photo mounts, handwritten labels, or simple inked borders, will impart a sense of nostalgia and make an inspiring display.

KEEPSAKES

In the age before e-mail, instant messaging, or even the telephone, keeping locks of hair or letters to remind you of a loved one was common practice. You can resurrect such sentimental but appealing customs by tying a lock of a relative's hair with ribbon and securing it in an envelope mounted on the page, or by mounting lines from a favorite letter alongside an image of the giver or sender.

SEPIA TINTING

Most materials will fade if exposed to strong sunlight. Try taping some colored papers and new photographs to the inside of a south-facing window pane. Leave undisturbed for a few weeks and let nature take its course. The photographs will yellow a little and the papers will fade, providing some "fake" vintage materials to work with.

You can also cover a sheet of colored paper with strips of flat decorative lace trimming or the edges of a paper doily, then expose to sunlight as before. The areas not covered by the lace or doily will leave a decorative pattern. Cut the patterned paper into strips and use to create borders and frames.

COLOR TINTING

Before color photographs were widely available, photographers would tint images by hand. Today you can color modern black-and-white images (or photocopies) in this way to add a touch of old-world charm. Although specialized tinting inks are available from photographic suppliers, you can use ordinary colored inks or acrylics. The step-by-step instructions in the panel below show how to do it.

STAGING

Why not try your hand at the "cut and paste" technique? Gather a collection of family photographs in fairly simple poses—seated or standing—then cut around the figures carefully with a craft knife. Arrange the cut-outs in a typically traditional pose: the head of the family standing, the mother seated with a small child sitting on her lap while other siblings stand or sit in the foreground, for example. Fix the group onto a traditional-looking background, perhaps found in a magazine or even in one of your own photos, then photocopy it onto photographic paper for an authentic monochromatic look.

Another idea for staging is to take an old family portrait photograph and substitute all the older members with cut-outs of your own family.

Spend time looking over old photo albums created by past family members. This will give you ideas and inspiration for your family scrapbook.

COLOR TINTING A BLACK-AND-WHITE PRINT

1 For a thin consistency, use colored inks direct from the bottle or dilute acrylic paints with water. Remove any excess from the brush prior to application and experiment on a discarded photograph to gauge results.

2 Your ink layers should resemble a wash. Avoid heavy colors and opt instead for soft subtle tones and a maximum of three colors. These should be applied with a soft artist's brush, using just the tip.

3 The idea is to highlight specific areas that you wish to draw attention to, such as lips, eyes, and hair, or in this case, the boy's dungarees, which have been softly washed with green. Try different combinations of highlighted details to find one that works.

preserving the past

Old family photographs are often left in storage, out of sight, so they may be damaged when they are retrieved; or there may be no record of who the subjects are. But with some repair and detective work, you'll have valuable images for your album.

If you want to include original photos already showing signs of wear and tear, don't repair the image: you may damage it further. Never use sticky tape to restore torn edges—this will mark and discolor the photo over time. Instead, place fragile originals in small transparent (acid-free) sleeves to prevent any handling damaging their fragile surfaces or catching loose corners. These clear sleeves can also act as a decorative device when secured with an attractive length of ribbon or twine.

Photocopying precious pictures or newspaper articles enables you to display them without fear of damage to the original, and can also be used to blow up and highlight specific details that may otherwise go unnoticed by the viewer. Such details can also be annotated, if any extra information can be gleaned from older

relatives. For example, a 1920s portrait of a little girl in an elaborate lacy dress will be enhanced by a note reading, "Great Aunt Lucy says this was her everyday outfit!" If you annotate old pictures, write carefully with a fountain pen in keeping with the age of the photograph.

MOUNTING

It is very important to avoid modern adhesives when mounting your older images on your scrapbook pages because these can seep through the delicate paper and cause staining. The proper (and careful) way to mount photographs is with traditional photo mounts, as described on page 10. These small—usually self-adhesive— triangular pockets neatly slip over each corner of the photograph and instantly add a touch of old-world charm.

USING A COMPUTER TO REPAIR A DAMAGED PICTURE

 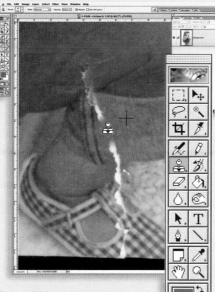

1 Blemishes, discoloration, and fading can all be improved through digital retouching. Even missing areas can be reinstated by using the cloning tool to sample pixels from similar sections to fix the area.

2 Small blemishes or unwanted marks and stains can often be removed by simply dabbing the cloning brush over the affected area, using pixels located next to the blemish or mark.

3 Most popular image-editing programs will feature automatic correction tools (Auto Enhancing, Auto Fix, or Auto Correction). These tools let you analyze the color, tone, and brightness of the image, then remix to create an ideal balance.

COMPUTER MANIPULATION

Recent advances in computer technology mean that many of us now have the facilities to transfer images onto our hard drive where they can be stored and retrieved safely and easily. Scanning original pictures can produce excellent results. Also, the image can be manipulated as well as digitally stored. Improving the quality and look of photographs is simply a matter of making a few fine alterations using the scanner's own software or an on-screen image-editing program (see the step-by-step instructions above).

EYEWITNESS ACCOUNTS

Take time to chat with older members of the family and take note of their stories. Older people often have an encyclopedic knowledge of family members and all the complex relationships between different branches of the family. Use their information to identify mystery sitters and give them their proper place in your family story. Their eyewitness accounts of historical events and everyday life will also give you valuable insights into past times and help bring the pages of your album to life.

MEMORABILIA

Preserving keepsakes—such as newspaper clippings, used tickets for a journey, and old postcards—in your scrapbook gives extra atmosphere and authenticity to your pages. However, you are less likely to have ephemera from your grandparents' time than from your own, so be inventive. Ask your older relatives for memorabilia or find on the Internet one of the many companies that now supply copies of old newspapers for specific dates, as well as other old ephemera that can be matched to events as appropriate.

ancestral profile

Dedicating a few pages in your scrapbook to profiling just one person from an earlier generation can be a highly rewarding experience both for you and for future readers in your family.

Letters and documents can help you chart the lives of your older relatives, almost like piecing together a family puzzle.

Not only does an ancestral profile provide a permanent record for those yet to come, but you will also become engrossed in the details of a life and time intrinsically different from your own.

Before you start, think about the questions you would like answered when looking at someone else's photo collection. Usually you will want to know more about the person before you: who they were, how they lived, what they did, what kind of clothes they wore, whether they had a family, and what the significant events in their lives were. These are all questions that should be addressed within the pages of your album. Try to include photographs that depict all the stages of your subject's life—childhood, school days, army life, work, family life, and old age. These can then be supplemented with any images of their environment

you can find: their home, their place of work, or the area in which they lived.

In addition, supporting evidence such as official documents, newspaper clippings, letters, swatches of clothes (see the facing page), even eyewitness accounts of great events will help create a clearer and more complete profile of your subject.

One of the most striking ways to present an ancestral profile is to group a series of favorite portraits of your subject around a text panel outlining his or her life story. Embellish photos mounted onto the pages of your album with sophisticated hand-drawn silver or gold borders (see the step-by-step box). Otherwise, mount images on delicate cream or sepia-tinted papers reminiscent of those they would have originally been displayed with. Any leftover space can be filled with ephemera.

MOUNTING

You can signify the importance of certain documents by linking them directly to the related images—for example, mounting a baby photo onto a copy of a birth certificate or attaching a wedding photo to a wedding license.

LEISURE ACTIVITIES

Even if you don't have all the images you need, you can still construct a narrative around pleasurable pastimes. Sheets of music, a few photocopied record sleeves of tunes popular at the time, or membership cards from a club or society will help build up a picture of your ancestor's leisure time.

CHANGING FASHIONS

Clothing immediately dates any photograph, although a photo can never portray the detail or tactile nature of a fabric. If you have scraps of antique cloth or lace, or even a small item such as an embroidered handkerchief or napkin, mount them alongside your prints, or secure them in a clear sachet or envelope. Old fabric and patterns are strongly evocative, particularly when the clothing in the picture is black and white but the scrap placed alongside it on the page is vividly colored.

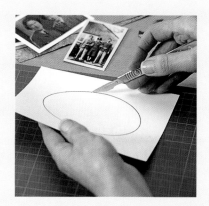

GOLD MOUNTS WITH WHITE BORDERS

1 With a craft knife, cut out an oval frame from white paper to go over the top of the profile and fix the white paper with photo mount corners (to preserve the old image).
2 Cut out another oval shape from the gold paper but this time measure and mark a larger oval cut-out. Make

sure the white paper frame shows through, giving a deep white perimeter border. Fix the gold paper onto the white with glue.
3 Using a craft knife, trim the edges of the gold mount carefully as desired (rounded corners or squared) and fix the image onto your album page.

creating a family tree

Compiling a detailed record of as many generations of your family as possible within the pages of your scrapbook will give future readers the clearest picture of their genealogical heritage.

Look in storage areas or archive boxes for information. Fish out what you need to tell a story through the pages of your album.

Genealogy has never been so popular, and there are now many ways to find relevant information. The Internet provides a quick and easy way to contact family and friends all over the world who may have images that are missing from your own personal collection. You can also use the Internet to find helpful genealogy sites to further your research in this area. However, the first port of call will generally be within your own immediate family. Look through relatives' photograph albums, because many will go back at least a few generations. Try to find birth certificates, letters, wartime documents, and wedding licenses since all will help make the connections between your ancestors clear. If relatives are reluctant to part with these treasures, simply photocopy them or scan them into a computer. The resulting images can then be used to carry out further research at your leisure, or to provide a decorative and informative element to your scrapbook.

You may wish to indulge the detective within you. Government agencies and local church records hold vast sources of historical data. Most official records are freely available, although it can often take some dedicated research to find the right department.

So how far should you go? Most of us begin delving into the past in order to learn more about our origins. The uncovering of our roots is usually more interesting than establishing that we have a sixth cousin twice removed living in some distant country. For the purposes of an album, charting the descendants of immediate family is probably the best course of action. Otherwise, a small family tree may turn into a neverending quest.

WEB LINKS

You can now perform a simple surname search on comprehensive search engines. However, this is likely to result in thousands of hits. There are methods to refine your search: try using a surname and the location you believe your family has roots in. Alternatively, try logging onto specific genealogy sites, as these have hundreds of differing resources. For serious exploration into your family history, go to "Researching your roots" (*pages 26–27*) for more information.

DECORATIVE DEVICES

Break up banks of images by including family mottoes and crests in your design. Investigate this subject on the Internet, or if you're feeling creative, why not design your own, using sayings or motifs that relate directly to your family?

LAYOUTS

The simplest form of family tree is a linear descendant tree in which all the descendants of the original couple are illustrated, using simple interconnecting lines. However, there is no reason why you could not turn this structure on its head, and base your tree on one of your children, or yourself, and trace backward. Another option—if you have a computer—is to check out software packages such as Family Tree Maker. This provides layout suggestions and design ideas for your family tree.

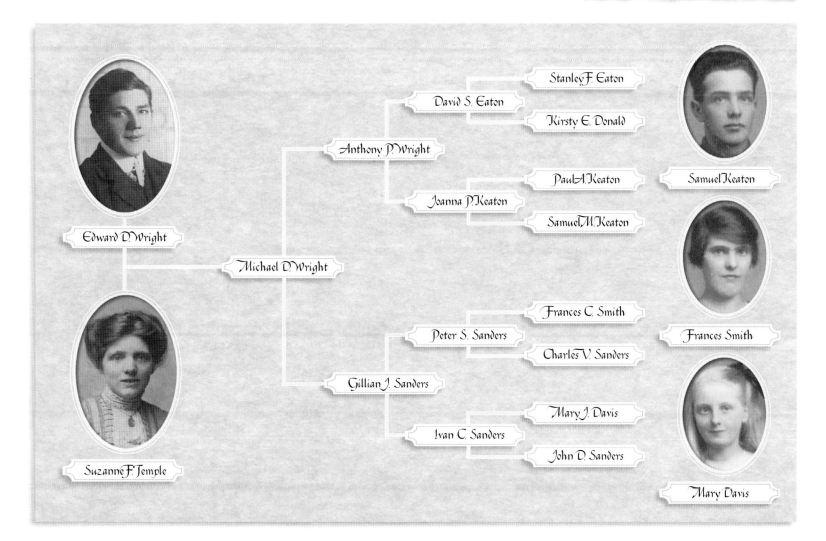

illustrating a family tree

If you are looking for a decorative way to portray the history of your family, a tree is the obvious motif that springs to mind. This device has long been used in traditional designs and provides a strong structure to work with.

Take a look through natural history books or magazines to get some idea of tree shapes and designs, then hand-draw a simplified version on the page in which your images will be set. You may find that this takes a little time, as you will have to work out in advance how many branches you need and the intersections required. Images or names of the earliest couple in your tree should be written in the trunk, while successive generations will be arranged in the branches above them. If your family has a huge number of branches, or if there are just too many images to make this a feasible option, you may need to simplify or "prune" the tree a little before you start.

To continue the tree motif, consider using an enlarged overall image of a single tree or woodland scene as a background on which to lay out your entire page. Turning down the contrast and increasing the brightness on your photocopier will enable you to produce a paler background that will not detract from your composition. Alternatively, you may wish to forgo the background imagery altogether.

It is worth considering overlaying or grouping specific generations in a montage. This will help emphasize a single unit within your family tree and make a far greater impact than simply framing the collection.

Whatever you decide, remember to allocate plenty of room for full names, dates, and places of birth and death if known. After all, you are laying down a piece of history that will be useful, as well as attractive, in the future.

A scattering of stylized leaves sprayed gold or silver plus white labels placed centrally make a decorative and informative family tree.

USING THE TREE DESIGN

The tree illustration on the opposite page is an example of a thematic way to depict your ancestry. Photocopy the sample and paste it into your scrapbook, then use a calligraphy ink pen or other decorative pen to write in your family names along the trunk. Then, taking the images you wish to display, cut them into shapes to fit the fruit at the ends of the branches. If you don't want to photocopy the tree, you can trace the sample and transfer the traced image onto your album page, coloring it in to match your overall page design.

1. _____
2. _____
3. _____
4. _____
5. _____
6. _____
7. _____
8. _____
9. _____
10. _____
11. _____
12. _____
13. _____
14. _____

researching your roots

Among your reasons for researching your ancestry will probably be a desire to know your "roots." Perhaps you want to discover if you're descended from a particular person or if you have links with another country.

Over the past several centuries, millions of people emigrated to the New World. Immigration records can help you trace your past.

As with any thorough genealogy research, a good starting place, after your family, is the Internet. Several web sites will enable you to trace as far back as the eighteenth century. If your ancestors came from abroad and you know their country (and preferably port) of origin and the approximate period of their arrival, then you're in a much better position to find relevant information.

Throughout history, people have left their country of birth and emigrated elsewhere. Between 1892 and 1924, over 22 million Americans came through Ellis Island and can trace their ancestry through the Ellis Island records office. Similarly, between 1831 and 1982, more than three million immigrants arrived in Australia. In Canada, from 1852 to 1977, over 11 million people entered the country. All these new arrivals were looking for a better life.

There are numerous web sites listing billions of names and including full details from government censuses. The more information you have, the better.

Remember, many European immigrants changed their surnames (shortening or Anglicizing them) after their arrival in order to "blend" in. So watch out for variant spellings, incorrect abbreviations, and other transcription errors that could hamper your search.

Alternatively, you may consider setting up your own web site and inviting others to participate. Including relevant keywords, such as names and places, will attract those who are using the same words as part of their own search.

Spending time unearthing your roots opens up a wealth of information and provides invaluable photos to chart this historical path.

CHARTING YOUR HERITAGE

With your research done, think carefully about how to include the most important findings within your album. Set aside a proportion of your page to trace ethnic origins. This can be approached as an independent element. Arranging images around a map of the relevant country—say, Ireland, Poland, or Italy—will help

set the scene, along with dates and details regarding those early settlers. Don't forget to leave space for documentation, as this is essential for telling the story.

USEFUL WEB SITES

Search under "genealogy" to bring up numerous links, or try:
Ellis Island:
www.ellisislandrecords.org
National Archives of Australia:
www.aa.gov.au
National Archives of Canada:
www.archives.ca

a new arrival

A birth in the family is sure to offer a rich seam of memories to treasure. From the excitement of the birth through the closeness of the days that follow, a well-made record is bound to become one of the most-thumbed sections of your family album.

Baby feet imprints scattered around can add a sweet touch to the page.

For most of us, the birth of a child is the most extraordinary experience of our lives, and we want to capture every detail for the future. But how many of us have a box tucked away crammed with photos of the newborn, personal mementos, and assorted data? Instead of leaving it all to gather dust, the contents can be used to make some of the most evocative pages in your family record—a full account of the arrival of your new family member. Cards, medical data, the incredibly minute identity tag from the new baby's ankle, even tiny pieces of ribbon from the first sweater or blanket—all can be pressed into service to make both a pretty and a meaningful record of the first few days.

However impromptu in composition, those hurried snapshots of a flustered and tired new mother in bed with a small red bundle are essential reminders of a special moment you won't want to forget. Don't discard them.

Everyone wants to be pictured with the new arrival—usually resulting in a series of delighted faces beaming adoringly at a bundle swaddled in a blanket. Choose the best picture of the newborn and place it in the center of the page in your scrapbook, then cut out all the beaming family members and friends and arrange them to form a frame around the brand-new member of your family circle. With first babies in particular, this will emphasize the fact that a new generation has come

COLOR TO BLACK AND WHITE

The first pictures of a newborn can sometimes be disappointing. Babies can be bruised by their passage into the world, so you might want to print color negatives in monotone to eliminate the less attractive part of your picture—your baby's reddened complexion—while catching his or her enchanting delicacy.

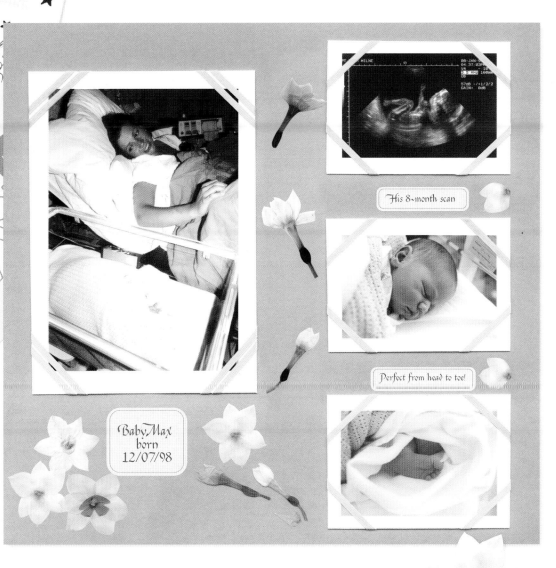

His 8-month scan

Perfect from head to toe!

Baby Max
born
12/07/98

into being with the new
life. If you want to give an elegant
feel to these pages, use sepia-effect
images to lend a touch of old-
fashioned charm (*see page 16*).

ANTICIPATING THE GREAT EVENT

Images of a smiling, expectant
mother, the baby shower, even the
ultrasound picture, combined with
photographs of your newborn baby,
will enable you to establish a
narrative leading up to the occasion
and help convey the feeling of
impending excitement.

USING SIZE AND COLOR

Take inspiration from the traditional
blue for a boy and pink for a girl and
color-coordinate your pages to match
your baby. Mount groups of images
on beautiful handmade papers to add
continuity, texture, and an extra
touch of artistry, and then paste the
page into your scrapbook.

A PRECIOUS LOCK OF HAIR

There is nothing quite so soft as
the hair of a baby. Cut off a lock and
tie a few strands together using a
piece of fine embroidery thread.
Finish this memento in a neat bow
and encase it in a transparent sachet
before mounting it on the page.

EMBOSSING

Available from crafts stores and thin
enough to be cut with scissors,
aluminum or copper sheeting is
perfect for making a striking header

for your page. To emboss the
aluminum or copper sheet, cut a
metal rectangle to size, then using a
spent ballpoint pen, write your
baby's name and date of birth on
the wrong side of the aluminum.
Write it backward, along the length
of the metal, pressing down with the
pen as hard as you can. When you
turn over the metal, the wording will
appear as an embossed imprint.
Finish the album page with a
decorative border that you have
created in the same manner.

*Using dried flowers in
your album pages will
bring color and delicacy
to the layout.*

baby naming

Of the many milestones in your children's lives that you wish to record for posterity, the celebration of a baby naming, bris, or christening will often be one of the first occasions. This important "welcoming" deserves a page in the family scrapbook.

Baby namings, brises, and christenings are times to formally acknowledge the naming of your child, welcome them into the world, and recognize your responsibility for their care and upbringing. It is important to remember this special time, and record an account of the day.

Although your child will inevitably take center stage on the page, remember to include photographs of family: grandparents, siblings, and aunts and uncles all help build a picture of the child's family and instill a sense of belonging. Formal shots may convey the importance of the event, but mix them with more casual shots when choosing your images. A proud father cradling his child, siblings whispering or playing together, and relatives catching up on family news create an overall image of the day.

Adding a picture of the place of the ceremony will set the scene, while images of a meal or party after the event will complete the narrative. Your aim is to create a unique collection that reflects the excitement and emotion of the whole occasion. Sometimes, creating an hour-by-hour countdown of the day will give a sense of the order of events. Try to find a special picture for each hour and use decorative devices, such as a clock motif.

WHAT'S IN A NAME?

Parents often spend a long time choosing a name for their child. Some names have meanings, or traditional or religious roots. Maybe the child

Charming items of baby ephemera, such as storks, diaper pins, and tiny baby bottles, help to create the right feel for a baby-naming page.

MAKING A FRAME FROM DOILIES

Adapt the more commonplace round designs, found in your local store.

1 Choose a doily that is larger than your photograph and place it on a flat surface. Position your photograph in the center of the design and mark the edges using a soft pencil.

2 Remove your photograph and use the pencil lines as a guide to draw a larger rectangle around the perimeter.

3 Cut around the outer lines to create your mount. To recreate the original undulating edges, use small sharp scissors and, following the pattern of the filigree design, cut away any unwanted areas. Then mount your photograph in the centrally marked position.

has been named after a relative, a friend, or even a famous person. Whatever the reason, it is a nice idea to add some explanatory text to the page to describe how and why the name was chosen.

LOVING LETTERS

Another way to personalize the page is to place your baby's initials along one edge of the album page. Cut the initials out of colored card or use illuminated stickers, then, alongside each initial, make a list of words beginning with that letter to describe your child, or find words that have a special meaning to you or your loved ones.

FRAMING DEVICES

For christening images, try using delicate paper doilies cut into rectangles as mounts, as their delicate filigree edges echo the lace found on a traditional christening gown (see the box above). Alternatively, use diaper pins to fix a photograph to a mount or to hold snippets of ribbon or fabric from the christening gown to the scrapbook page.

ALL IN THE DETAIL

Guests at a baby naming often give keepsake gifts for the child to enjoy when they get older. Make a list of who gave what so that the names will not be forgotten as the years pass.

Write the names neatly on the back of a four-inch square of pretty gift wrap paper, then fold the top and bottom edges to the center and crease. Repeat with both sides, folding them to the center and creasing. Tie the resulting parcel with a ribbon and fasten to the page with adhesive or other fixative. Untie the ribbon and open the parcel to reveal the names.

EPHEMERA

Incorporating memorabilia such as the order of service, lines from a song, invitation cards, and messages of goodwill helps to convey the importance of the occasion and bring happy memories flooding back.

coming of age

Our lives are often plotted around significant rituals and traditions. These may occur only once in a lifetime, such as 16th or 18th birthdays, a bar or bat mitzvah, or graduation day, and hence should be captured and preserved.

Graduation day, a symbol of adulthood, is one of our most memorable lifetime events.

Rituals are important to everyone, and those events that are never to be repeated hold a special place in your family album.

Graduation is an exciting time for a young adult. Often this is when the graduate is bursting with ideas, dreams, and plans for the future. A wish list is a great way to add interest to the page and can be used as a background or as text next to photos. This list of aspirations is also interesting to refer to in later years to see if any of the wishes came true.

This memorable day can also be tinged with sadness. The close-knit group of friends that you formed at college may never be reunited, so display your closest companions grouped by the context in which you met them. For instance, friends from the track team or the debating society could be grouped together on the page.

BORDERS AND MOUNTS

Caps and gowns will be the order of the day and will be shown in many of the photographs. Why not convey the flavor of the ceremony by fixing your photographs in place with small tassels and colored cord? You can also apply narrow strips of grosgrain ribbon down one edge of a photo and snip the lower end into a decorative "V" shape, then fix the ribbon to the page using colored sealing wax embossed with a stamp in one corner, perhaps bearing a date or initial or a suitable motif.

THAT WAS THEN

Include some fun "before and after" pictures of the graduates too. You could arrange a small gallery of extremely sophisticated cap-and-gown snapshots alongside the corresponding incoming freshman images for contrast.

COLORED RIBBON BORDERS

For a sophisticated effect around your photo, border a single image or even a number of images with different colored ribbons.

1 Lay your image in place on the page and use it as a guide to draw a larger rectangle around the perimeter to create a deep border. Repeat this process two more times if you're using three different-colored ribbons.

2 Remove the photograph and apply a thin layer of size (a specialized adhesive that can be purchased at any good craft store) within the border areas.

3 Your ribbon pieces should be measured to fit exactly in the three borders, and each colored piece cut into four strips for the edges. Make sure the corners come together diagonally. Smooth the ribbon with your hands and place the photo in the middle, fixing it with special tape or adhesive.

RELIGIOUS RITUALS

In the Jewish calendar, it is a boy's bar mitzvah and a girl's bat mitzvah that highlight a coming of age.
To capture this tradition, illustrate the notable elements of the ritual—the reciting of scripts, lighting of candles, and feasting—with a photo collage to build up the day's narrative.

MOTIFS

To set the tone for the page, draw an oversized candle up one side or in the center of the page and mount a picture of the child within the flame, or place a series of images on the candlestick. Mounting an extract from the religious ceremony will help portray the true meaning of the day, especially when juxaposed with an image of the child reading the script in the synagogue.

weddings

Out of all special occasions, getting married is one of the most significant. You will have no lack of photographs, but remember to present different mementos too—all will provide a rich source of cherished memories to look back on.

Have you ever spoken to a newly married couple about their wedding day? More often than not, they will say the day seemed to fly by in a happy blur. A detailed account of the day serves as a record for future generations so present recollections in a narrative alongside the images. What was the most touching moment? What was the favorite wedding gift?

Many people feel that they should display only the formal professional pictures taken on the big day, but those unposed incidentals, such as a bride or groom getting ready or a series of shots showing the bride leaving home and on her way to the ceremony, add charm and help tell a story (see the box on the opposite page). While it is also great to show

the scale of the occasion by incorporating large group shots, including close-up images helps capture the mood and fine detail of the day. An intricate hairstyle, the bridal bouquet, a guest's beautiful hat, or that symbolic band of gold on a bride's finger—all help illustrate the essence of the event.

It is often said that you should mount only perfect photographs, but

the best images aren't necessarily technically perfect. A slightly blurred image can convey the excitement of the moment, so bear this in mind when you are deciding whether to include or omit a picture. Don't be afraid either to include touches of humor: a photograph of a slightly disheveled bride collapsing into giggles can sum up just how enjoyable the day was.

Focusing in on an aspect of the day, like the bride's bouquet, can brighten and enliven your album. As flowers are perishable, it is important to have a visual record.

REVEALING DISPLAY

Capture the unfolding excitement by creating a concertina-style display.

1 Choose four or five pictures and place them in sequence on a sheet of paper, leaving about half an inch between each adjoining edge.

2 Glue the photographs firmly onto the paper and leave to dry.

3 Using the area of paper between each photograph as your fold lines, fold the entire length of paper back and forth, concertina-style, so that you end up with a single stack, then press flat.

4 Place the stack in position in your scrapbook and glue the last paper section to the page, leaving the remainder of the concertina loose, enabling you to pull out and reveal the entire sequence of pictures.

RETOUCHING

Lend a touch of old-fashioned romance to modern-day images by imitating tinted wedding portraits. Delicately applying photographic oil paints to black-and-white prints using cotton swabs, or a toothpick for small areas, will accentuate details like the flowers of the bridal bouquet.

CHAMPAGNE LOVE HEARTS

It is customary at weddings to toast the happy couple with champagne. To capture this within your album use two discarded cages from champagne corks and fashion them into tiny heart shapes, then mount the hearts side by side on a label steamed from the bottle or onto a photo of the bride and groom.

If these cork cages are a little too bulky for the album, use fine silver wire instead for an authentic alternative. Fashion two delicate heart shapes or the initials of the bride and groom, then place them together on a background of scraps of gift wrap paper or again onto labels steamed from champagne bottles. The date of the wedding can also be written in fine wire, perhaps with the addition of tiny beads for decoration, then fixed to the page with dots of adhesive.

COLLECTED EPHEMERA

As with all special events, save room for keepsakes. The sheet of paper with the order of the service, lace from the bridal veil, newspaper announcements, a delicate envelope mounted and filled with confetti—these all make delightful additions.

FRAMING

Adorning the edges or corners of significant images with a few pressed and dried petals from the bridal bouquet or bridesmaids' posies provides a simple yet romantic way to frame favorite photographs and adds to the sense of occasion.

birthday parties

Whether the party pictures you took show the guests in their best finery or—particularly good for a scrapbook page—in costume for a costume party, they often give you excellent material with which to get creative.

Birthday party invitations are often cleverly designed. If you're thinking of making a themed birthday-party page in your scrapbook, try arranging cut-outs of the revelers in their costumes alongside the original party invitation. You can simply arrange the photos in a straightforward way around the invitation or cut out pictures of the guests and overlap them with the edges of the invitation, so it looks as though the party is overflowing onto your album page.

If you have pictures of a costume party, devise a "lift the flap" picture. Experts in the art of disguise will love this fun way to display a party photo. Cut around the face of the guest in the photo, leaving ¼ inch (5mm) uncut on one side to act as a flap hinge, then stick a picture of their everyday face behind it (one without the mask, makeup, fake beard, or other costume elements). Just lift the flap to see who it is.

CHILDREN'S PARTIES

Creating a page to commemorate a child's birthday party in your scrapbook can be an activity for both you and the little ones. Choose simple shapes that small hands can cut out—like triangles cut from greeting cards to mimic party hats—and get your helpers to string the shapes together on a length of colored cord, then fasten one end of the cord to each side of the page so that the line of decoration hangs across the page like bunting. Fix little pictures—of party guests or the birthday cake—to each triangle. If the triangles are left to hang free

REMOVING RED EYE

A red-eye retouching pen, available from camera specialists, will remove red eye on existing prints. Alternatively, it is possible to improve images using a fine felt-tip pen, but be careful not to remove that essential white highlight within the eye, or your sitter could take on a demonic expression!

from the cord, you can write names, dates, or any other information on the back. Include gift wrap, lengths of party streamer, and unused balloons to add color and vitality to the page.

COOKIE LABELS

If you are using cutters to make cookies for a children's party, also use them to create unusual labels in your album. Use sheets of colored paper and simply draw and cut around each cutter, then add your comments—or ask the children to add theirs.

DECORATIVE DEVICES

Include champagne labels in your design for an adult party, or try enlarging or reducing memorabilia and then placing it around the edges of your pages to form a decorative border. You can combine various sizes to create artistic montages. Include a relevant birth sign along with the day's horoscope. If the horoscope is photocopied from a newspaper, tint an uninspiring monochrome print with watercolor, or photocopy it onto pretty colored paper so it fits in with the page.

NUMBERS

Birthdays are all about getting one year older, so the number theme is an obvious one! Cut out numbers from old birthday cards (either outside or inside the card), newspapers, or magazines. Or try stickers or stamps and make a neat row or rows of the same number in as many different typefaces you can find. This has a great effect as a border or background.

SILHOUETTES

Take a tip from the Victorians and create a cameo-style profile to use as a charming, old-fashioned heading for a memorable birthday page.

1 Pose your subject in profile against a plain, light-colored wall. Make sure facial features are well-defined and arrange long hair in a ponytail or bun to accentuate the profile. Take a photo.

2 When the image is developed, photocopy and enlarge it (if required) before cutting out the head and neck. Take care with the nose and mouth.

3 Place the image on a sheet of dark-colored paper. Draw around the image and then cut out your finished profile.

4 Cut a simple oval shape from pastel-colored card or paper and mount the profile on it before placing it in your scrapbook.

fun festivals

Children of all ages look forward to celebrations such as Halloween, Valentine's Day, and civic holidays. These events, occurring annually, may not appear to be defining moments in our lives, but most leave us with memories of precious time spent with family.

Include Valentine's Day cards and record the giver's name and date with a silver pen. You can also mount simplified silhouettes of hearts or cupids cut from colored card.

Children choosing—and making—their Halloween costumes, making Valentines, and watching colorful fireworks exploding are often captured in photographs that you can use in your album. There are also plenty of motifs and ephemera to go with these traditions.

ARRANGEMENTS

As you sort through your images of a festival like Halloween, you will probably find that many images lend themselves to sequence arrangements, such as carving the pumpkin or getting dressed up. Alternatively, create a colorful collage to illustrate the various designs of jack-o-lanterns or myriad costumes. Whatever devices you choose, always leave space for valuable details that sum up the day—the awe on a child's face, a detail of a costume, or a little one overcome with sleep but still splendid in a charming costume.

VALENTINE DISPLAYS

What a wonderful opportunity to include heart-shaped everything! Heart-shaped stickers or paper cut-outs sprinkled liberally over the page will set the scene, and whether this page in your scrapbook is a way to remember a special Valentine's Day or a gesture to a loved one, the possibilities are great. Try novel and amusing ways to represent the two people involved in the love match: take two playing cards (the King and Queen of Hearts, of course) and make your own version of the cards. Use colored papers and add your couple's faces in place on the King and Queen. Different colored foil candy papers will add three-dimensional decorative interest to a display page, particularly when fashioned into tiny heart shapes.

CROPPING

If you find that you have many similar images within your collection or odd photographs that do not merit

mounting, do not discard them. Cut out pictorial elements such as pumpkins, bobbing apples, a smiling face, or a costume for Halloween; or for Valentine's Day, cut out flowers, cuddly toys, red heart shapes, or romantic gift items and scatter them around the page. If you have blurred images of fireworks against a night sky, consider enlarging them to use as an abstract backdrop on which to mount your close-ups of people enjoying the fun.

FRAMING

The tradition of trick-or-treating ensures your children will return home happy and laden with candies. Instead of throwing away the wrappers, smooth them out and use them behind photographs to create decorative mounts. Use your imagination in arranging the frame: here, the eyes on two candy wrappers have been used to echo the cat's eyes on the bag in the picture.

CHOCOLATE FUDGE

LIQUORICE
Soft Caramel

Kirsty with her spoils!
Halloween 2003

religious celebrations

Annual events like Easter, Hanukkah, and Christmas are special times when family and friends gather, sometimes from far afield, to celebrate. Highlights include family traditions and special menus.

The message behind many religious celebrations can often be lost in a whirl of commercialism, so aim to include information about the true meaning of the celebrations, as well as the fun side. Often, the only time families see a cousin, aunt, or grandparent is around Christmas or Easter, so make your page special to your family by including little reminders of what the celebration means to you by adding text from songs or readings to family photographs. Include any images you have of a sumptuous table setting, the Christmas tree in all its glory, and memorabilia such as nativity play programs.

Most religious celebrations have their own instantly recognizable symbols, so be sure to include some of these when considering the display of your memories relating to a special celebration or ceremony. For example,

you can use a Menorah for Hanukkah, the ubiquitous egg for Easter, and a wealth of religious and decorative elements for Christmas.

DECORATIVE DEVICES

Backing an entire page with gift wrap will instantly inject a festive touch to your layout, while attaching unused gift tags offers you space on the busy background to write dates, names, and any witty anecdotes you may remember from the day. Or place a picture of your mealtime near a traditional recipe that is a family favorite.

THEMED SHAPES AND CUT-OUTS

Use leftover foil wrappers from Easter candy and cut out a family of tiny chicks to decorate your page—dot them around as if hopping about. You can also display family photos

Christmas Cake
2 containers candied cherries
1 container candied mixed citrus peel

Use recipes, festive cards, and photos of the meal to show the themes of the day.

in a fan shape on the page. Cut three or four favorite portraits into egg shapes, and cut a matching oval cover for each in colored card. Gather the covers and the portraits together in a neat egg-shaped stack, then fix it onto your album page using a brass paper fastener pushed through all the layers of portraits and card covers at the top of the egg shape. Next, fan out the shapes from the swivel point so that each portrait is covered by its cover. The reader can rotate each cover around to reveal the portrait beneath.

GATHERING OF THE CLANS

If your family is scattered geographically, set aside room on the page to describe where each member has traveled from. For an innovative style of labeling, cut different-size circular festive baubles from thin card. Decorate them with simple zigzag lines and paint each of the sections in a different color. When the baubles are dry, further define the lines with a black pen before adding the written details you want to include within the most central section, using a metallic pen.

STAMPING

Many Christmas cards have raised surfaces—perhaps the outline of a Christmas tree, a star, Santa Claus, or a snowman. You can use these to create decorative stamps with which to liven up your album page. Simply paint the raised surface with a thin layer of water-based paint, then press it firmly onto the page of your album, using a slight rocking motion to ensure that all areas come into contact with the paper. Lift it cleanly away to reveal the imprint. Repeat your pattern around the page.

FRAMING

Instead of throwing away those old Christmas cards, cut out decorative borders and use them to frame individual prints. Alternatively, you could use glitter or strips of festive bunting, self-adhesive stars, or snowflakes. These will all make great borders. Cut out special messages that people have written in cards and place them alongside the border, forming an overall picture of a special celebration.

the family

While we all look forward to special occasions, it is the way we lead our everyday lives that will interest people in years to come. Many of our happiest memories are of commonplace activities and there are numerous ways to capture this ordinary life.

Think about what appeals to you most when you look at old photos or albums. Often it is the everyday images of people at play, rather than those formal occasions when everyone is on their best behavior. In an ever-changing world, pictures of relatives from as little as fifty years ago can somehow seem strangely exotic to us now—the cars they drove, the furniture in their homes, their leisure activities, and the way they dressed are all fascinating. Finding photos that record scenes from everyday life—such as a family breakfast, a new car, or something as simple as dad reading the newspaper—will have the same effect on future generations. Incorporating candid, unposed shots of family members going about their everyday business will enable you to add a lighthearted element to your album and will provide a welcome contrast to more formal pages.

Ordinary chores become intriguing when pictured in a previous time, so display pictures of chores for a future generation.

MEMORY QUILT

Create a patchwork quilt of family and friends. Cut photographs into squares, triangles, or diamond shapes, then arrange them on a sheet of colored paper in a traditional patchwork pattern. Allow a little space between each picture for the background to show through. Paste the whole sheet into your album.

ENLIVENING THE SCENE

Grouping photographs of one subject together is an excellent way of adding interest. Consider using a sequence of photos of the same subject to show excitement, movement, or humor. Several shots of a child running around or dressing up in a parent's clothes

DIARY FORMATS

Take inspiration from magazine layouts by including a photo story in your album. It is a great way of telling a story about everyday events, such as a typical weekend at home. Having laid out your sequence of photos, simply cut speech bubbles from paper and glue them in place, then write in the dialogue either by hand or by using a computer script font.

will bring the subject to life and create a cinematic effect. Or show the first car or a beloved bicycle to conjure up memories of youth.

COMIC STRIP

Go for a real comic-strip effect by mixing and matching photos. Cut out a number of head shots of family members. Look through pictures of everyday events and see if you can make any amusing substitutions. Maybe place grandma's head on a photo of dad watering the garden, dressed only in shorts; or stick baby's

head onto an image of mother cooking dinner. Shrink and enlarge photocopies of the images as required to get a "realistic" finished effect.

PHOTOFITS

Alternatively, you can create a rogues' gallery using photographs of family members. Choose photos in which the heads are a similar size and facing forward; better still if the subjects are making funny faces! First, cut each face into three equal sections: the first section should include the eyes and crown of the head; the second,

the nose; and the third the mouth and chin. Mix and match the pieces to create an entirely new family.

NEW DIMENSIONS

Bring mundane images to life with actual items. A picture of dad reading the paper becomes far more interesting when set alongside the article he was so engrossed in. An image of a child going to bed can be accentuated with a photocopy of a page from his or her favorite book, or the Sunday dinner enriched with the inclusion of a favorite family recipe.

house & garden

We all have pictures of our home in our albums, even if it is simply an incidental background in a family grouping. But have you ever thought of dedicating a page or two in your scrapbook to the place where you spend the vast majority of your life?

How often have you decorated a room or landscaped a garden and not been able to convey your sense of satisfaction at this achievement? Recording these images, and those of the creative process, will provide a lasting testament to all your hard work. Your home and garden are a reflection of personal preferences, and provide a reminder of the things your family requires to create a secure and welcoming environment.

When choosing pictures for your album, include details such as the corner of a room or individual items alongside overall shots. A favorite cushion, that plant you managed to grow from a seedling, a chair you have re-covered, or a treasured gift from a loved one: all these details make up a complete picture of your home and the things that matter to you.

As well as the house and garden, feature people or pets in some of your selected pictures; otherwise, a series of shots devoid of life can appear static. Include snapshots showing family members relaxing or going about their daily chores to help portray your house and garden as they are used, naturally. You could also show your pets dozing in their favorite sleeping place.

TIME-LAPSE PHOTOGRAPHY

Create an ongoing story by grouping a number of pictures on the same subject. For instance, you could show the various stages of a house-extension being built, a single room as it changes over the years, or a

Building my
Blissful
Bathroom

The Bathroom—
Untouched!

"Before" Floorboards

"After" Floorboards

Show the inspiration for your home design scheme by laying out the album pages like a designer's sample board, with paint samples, fabric, and wallpaper swatches.

garden during different seasons. Make a note of where you were standing when you took the first photograph and use the same position for the rest so as to make the images as similar as possible. This will not only link the group but will also help highlight the changes.

SAMPLE BOARDS

Planning a new decor (indoors or out) is probably the most exciting part of transforming a home or garden. Professional designers use sample boards to make their plans. On the board they might include pictures of any fixtures and fittings that will remain after the makeover, paint samples, swatches of fabric or wallpaper, and even abstract items like leaves or feathers to help create the mood they have in mind. Why not lay out your scrapbook to look like a sample board? It will provide a unique insight into the thought process behind the finished look and act as a permanent reminder of the intensity of color and textures used, long after the room has changed.

UP THE GARDEN PATH

Record your hours of hard labor in the garden by using seed packets as photo frames. Replace the pictures on the packets with your own garden snapshots so that readers will see your prize tomatoes or blooming flower beds. You can also place some pressed flowers alongside them. Use old

garden plans or sketches as background material and, in keeping with the theme, use plant labeling sticks as frames or borders or tie photos to the page with tiny bows of garden twine.

Write memorable dates of successes ("first tomato") or failures ("slug attacks of 2003") on plant labeling sticks, then glue to the page to add interest. Reflections and afterthoughts always provide interesting material for little dialogue boxes or labels.

THEMED CUT-OUTS

Cut photographs of the garden into leaf or flower shapes, then overlap them slightly when gluing them to the page to form a flower shape. Or for a page dedicated to the home, use keys, keyholes, or even mini-house shapes on which any relevant comments can be written (for example, documenting when the family first moved there).

BEFORE AND AFTER

Everyone loves a makeover, so include "before and after" shots and, if possible, images of the work in progress. These can be laid out in sequence, or you could enlarge the photo of the finished room or garden, then overlay the "before and intermediate" shots to create a unified whole. Attach the photos using small tabs of special tape on the parts that do not overlap.

Jordan takes his first bath by himself. A close encounter of the sink kind.

childhood firsts

Children grow up in the blink of an eye and those first-time events—like the first bath, first tooth, first steps, first birthday party—pass by regularly. Capturing these landmarks in your album creates an enduring record of an all-too-brief childhood.

As any parent knows, a child encounters many new experiences in the course of just one day. These milestones arise in many forms—the tears of frustration over a new task, those comical moments when introducing new tastes or making a first new friend, and the pure delight and surprise of the previously unknown. All should be reflected within the pages of your scrapbook. You could use themes (food, clothes, or skills) or categorize and group images on the page by significant years when "first" times happened. Alternatively, try mounting a collection of photo firsts on an old height chart. The labels can feature the child's age and be pasted next to his or her measurement.

ADDING DETAILS

Alongside traditional photographic images, consider adding humorous and personal touches such as photocopies of well-loved cartoon characters, pieces of a once-favorite mobile or jigsaw, charming hand prints, or a worn piece of a favorite blanket. Incorporating lines from a favorite first story book will immediately take you back in time and create warm memories. Use photocopied or handwritten lines from the book. Arrange them in the area around or adjacent to the child's photograph.

FIRST WORDS

A creative way to record your child's first word is to cut out letters from a newspaper and spell out the word several times with different typefaces going across both pages. If you want to set out a whole first phrase or sentence, you could arrange cut-out letters to spell the key words just once, angling the letters. Either treatment will look like a ransom note; add a date, so you have a record of when the word or phrase was spoken.

FIRST TOY

Focusing attention on a particular item, such as a favorite first toy, and enlarging this part of an image to enhance its importance to your child will instill a change of pace to the page. You can enlarge the area on a photocopier and print it at 20 percent tint. You could ask your child to make his or her own choice of detail to be enlarged, then use the resulting image as an atmospheric background for other pictures.

FIRST PAINTING

This precious artifact may be a large sheet of paper, daubed with paint and glitter; in fact, it may be too large for the scrapbook. In this case, you'll need to reduce the size of the painting. Make a color photocopy of it and then fold it neatly and glue it to the album page. In this way, you can can include the artwork in your scrapbook without damaging the real thing.

STEPPING OUT

Emphasize the significance of first steps by mounting pictures of your child walking. For an illusion of movement, arrange the photos as if your child were advancing toward the camera. Include the ones when they fell over as well! Alternatively, add motion to a single image with a series of small footprints traveling around the snapshot or going across a corner of the page.

GROWTH SPURTS

Start compiling an album of your child in his first year. Then photograph your child on the same day each year, and supplement each image with details of height, weight, and so on to create a comprehensive record. This album can include memorable dates like the first time your youngest child reaches an elder brother's height or the first time he measures four feet high!

RECORDED MEMORIES

No one ever forgets the first time their child counts to ten or recites the alphabet, so why not record these treasured sounds on video and transfer to a CD? Once encased in a clear sleeve or envelope, the CD can be dated and mounted on the page. Alongside the envelope, you could attach a list of your child's first spoken words and phrases. Write the real spelling alongside a phonetic version of the way he or she pronounced them.

school days

Days at school form some of the biggest moments in a child's life, and in a parent's, too. They signify an exciting period in your child's development when they are constantly learning and making new friends.

Use self-adhesive gold stars or good conduct stickers to create visual interest and a lively page border.

A child's time at school may stretch over many years, but generally we record only the early experiences during the formative years on film. Displaying what is often a very disjointed group of pictures in an attractive and coherent manner can be a struggle, however. But keep in mind that the aim of this page is to relive the strongest memories of being at school, and you'll be sure to make a creative and touching display.

Arranging and grouping together images in accordance with age or school years will, of course, help guide you through the years. In addition, your child's memorabilia will bring the pages to life. Include items such as drawings, written exercises, report cards, and a scrap of fabric taken from a first school sweatshirt or from a team sweater to help create an all-encompassing picture of your child's activities and progress during their time at school.

You will probably have a host of formal school portraits—of your child and her class—which act as a useful visual aid. You may also have taken your own snapshots at occasions such as the school play, sports events, or fundraisers. Don't be afraid to juxtapose these casual shots of your child interacting with other students with static portraits, as they will provide a pleasing contrast to the formality and inject an element of fun into the overall layout.

MINI MATCHBOOKS

Matchbooks saved from a hotel make charming booklet frames for small photos. Remove the matches, glue a photo of your child on top of the front flap, then glue another picture of him or her inside. The flap can be tucked into the book and opened by the reader to reveal the second picture.

DECORATIVE DEVICES

A simple addition to the page, like a sprinkling of gold stars or good

The printed name labels stuck inside school sweatshirts can be an effective decorative device for labeling.

conduct stickers that a child may have earned at school, will effectively break up a large bank of photographs and help draw the eye into the page. You could also add a touch of humor with graphic ink-blot stains (to resemble the splodges of ink that come from a traditional ink pen).

FRAMING

Pictures from art class and written exercises not only add a personal touch but can be used to mount individual photos or groups of images. A simple crayon border around a photo echoes the medium used by every child in the classroom. Alternatively, use lengths of cloth name tag (similar to those shown next to the photograph on page 48) to make interesting frames for an entire page or individual photos, giving readers a tactile memory of school days as well as a pictorial one.

LABELING

School calendars provide the ideal device for creating a running narrative. Photocopies of key dates from the school calendar let you signpost images and create an informative display. Make sure you include the names of all those school friends in photos—plus nicknames. (Otherwise, you may find that in years to come your child can't remember who they were.)

CREATIVE COLLAGE

Creating a colorful collage of photographs and collected memorabilia, such as paintings, drawings, a first signature, or simple sums, adds an essential designer element while enabling you to mount numerous disjointed images in a highly decorative manner. Most children, proud of their growing abilities, will be delighted to help create "their own" pages in the family album.

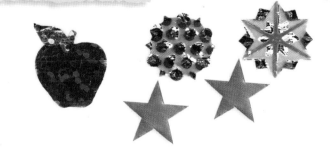

making an impact

Not all of us will have a rich source of material for all the people we want to include in our album. Think about using a scant number of images in more striking and original ways to give them impact on your pages.

It is possible to create a stimulating and visually entertaining layout with very few photographs, so don't be disheartened if your collection is lacking. Consider how you can capitalize on what you have. Take a look through decorating magazines, which frequently feature articles on displaying and arranging smaller numbers of pictures. These ideas can often be adapted to suit the pages of your album. Art and design books are also a useful source of information.

If in doubt, remember that often the simplest ideas work best. Mounting your photographs onto large rectangles of decorative card will significantly improve a layout. The resulting wide borders enhance the size of the prints and draw the eye toward the image. Using brightly colored backgrounds will instantly add depth and intensity to a few faded images, while the addition of a number of well-placed text boxes bursting with invaluable facts and figures will create an informative and eye-catching display.

LAMINATING

If you have some particularly delicate photographs, you can prevent them from falling apart by having them laminated. Most good photographic stores provide this service.

LABELING

Try your hand at origami. There are many simple yet stunningly effective models that require nothing but a small square of thin paper. What better way to display a limited number of photos than by supplementing them with witty labels written on windmills, flowers, or the classic crane? Also try using charcoal or wax crayon rubbings from old coins and medals, or blown-up specific photo details, such as quirky hats or dainty boots.

POP ART TRANSFORMATION

Pop art provides the perfect medium for playing with a single image and adding a colorful interpretation to an old print. This picture, in a pop-art style reminiscent of that of Andy Warhol, has been made from multiple copies of the same image, colored in various dramatic shades.

1 Choose the image you would like to manipulate. As you can see from the example, it works well to select a picture with features in quite close range.

2 To transform the image, you can either use a computer or photocopy the image onto acetate and roughly color the back of the acetate with bright acrylic paints.

3 Before arranging your layout, take a look at some Warhol prints. You could repeat the same colored image throughout, as in his famous Marilyn Monroe picture; you could graduate the shades to create a progression; or just go for vibrant contrasts, as shown here.

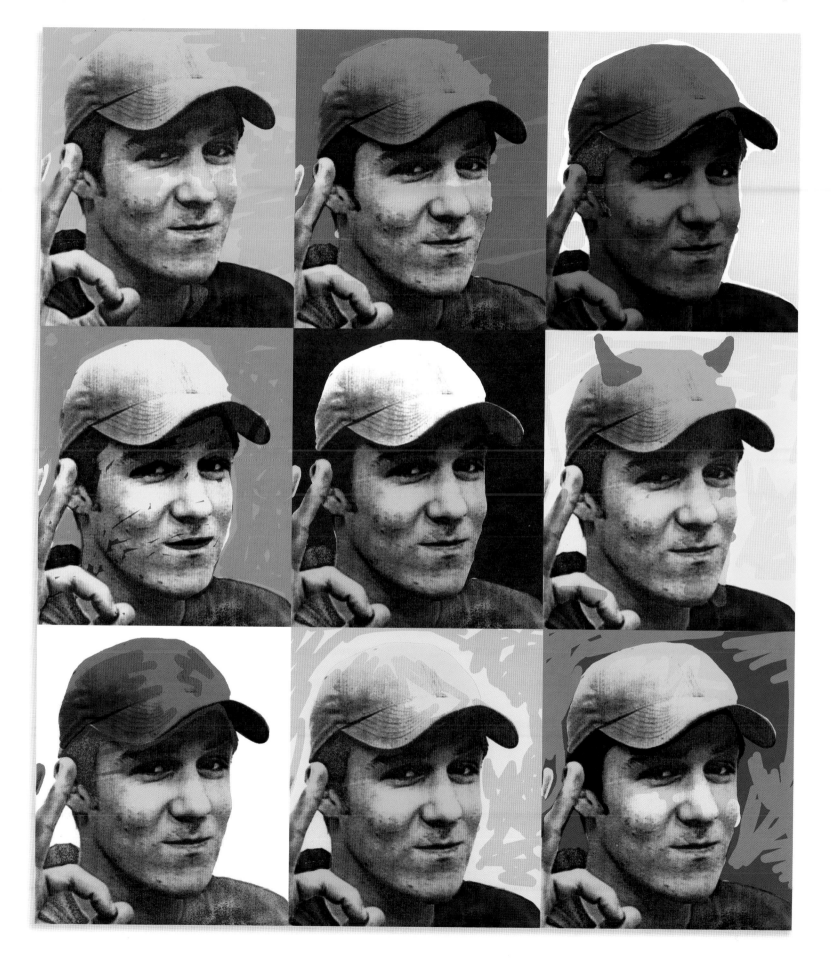

special trips

We all enjoy traveling abroad and encountering different cultures. Once we return to everyday life, we can relive the fun through our pictures of exotic beaches, mountain treks, or city explorations.

Photographs play an important role in reliving vacation experiences and remembering friendships forged while far from home. However, we tend to pack so much into these treasured trips that many details, place names, and events become lost in time and we are left with a jumble of photographs that we struggle to identify. It is important to impart as much information on the page as possible when displaying vacation snapshots—places, dates, and anecdotes will all help to conjure up a fuller picture of an area visited. Choosing a particular photo that symbolizes the vacation for you, to headline your page, will help draw people into the album, while arranging images by theme or area will create a natural flow. Framing pictures emphasizes special moments or places. Use marker pens or inks to create colored borders, and pick out a predominant color in the group—perhaps blue, if there are a lot of water-based images—to add interest and continuity.

COMIC MOMENTS

Consider having a page of comical snapshots, such as the time you got soaked in a tropical storm or the shot that makes it look as though the Eiffel Tower is growing out of your friend's head. If you can find some pictures of a stockade at an old fort or a "Wanted Dead or Alive" poster, you could create a modern-day pastiche. Take some favorite images of your friends or family and reduce or enlarge them with a photocopier before affixing their heads to the postcards to create a unique scene of your own.

HISTORIC LANDMARKS

It's sometimes difficult to capture a historic sight or fabulous view in its entirety without a wide-angled

Colorful foreign banknotes and unusual coins will add local atmosphere to your page.

Back photographs with pages from an old passport or photocopy the central page motif to make labels for your pictures. The passport page pattern will supply an instant reminder of travel to far-off, exotic locations.

TRAVEL COLLAGE

Juxtapose a small collection of postcards, tickets, coasters, leaflets, and even candy wrappers with your vacation snapshots to add depth to your page. Arrange them loosely to get the effect you want before sticking them down. Try to capture the flavor of your trip, whether it was cultural, scenic, exotic, or pure hectic fun.

camera lens—so cheat! Use a postcard instead then add a cut-out of yourself or a family member. Think scale here, so imagine your child towering over the Pyramids at Giza with bucket and spade in hand!

PICTURE FAN

Too many special trip photos to choose from? If you have a contact sheet then the answer is simple; just choose your favorite picture to use full size as a background. Next, cut the contact sheet into strips and fix all the pieces together (at one end) in your scrapbook using a paper fastener. The strips can then be spread out like a fan to view all the different shots from the vacation. Or you can make two fans and place one at the top left and one at the bottom right of the main picture.

PLOTTING A COURSE

Charting specific trips or events along a route will help bring back memories of your journey and serve as a guide to the images on the page. Simply hand-draw the route of your journey and highlight the points or places that correspond to certain pictures. Add labels, admission tickets, and other memorabilia collected on your trip.

DECORATIVE DEVICES

Menus, hotel business cards, local postcards, even visa or passport stamps help break up large expanses of photographs and also make attractive additions in their own right. You could back a group of photographs with pages from an old passport, or photocopy the central page motif to create artistic labels, since their distinctive design immediately denotes travel to distant places. Mounting colorful and diverse foreign bank notes or taking rubbings from loose change, using wax or charcoal sticks, will also add flavor and interest to your album.

vacations

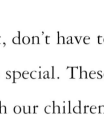

Vacations, long or short, don't have to involve a trip to an exotic clime to be special. These family trips provide memories of a time with our children that we will treasure long after they have flown the nest.

Add some postcards to your vacation spread as these add to the mood of the page.

Whether it be a week by the beach, a few days at a favorite theme park, or time spent in the country, these happy times provide us with unlimited photographs and plenty of images of joyful smiling faces.

When choosing your vacation snapshots, it is all too easy to concentrate on family members; be sure to include shots of your accommodation and any landscapes or places of interest you may have taken. These will help create a sense of your surroundings and place your family pictures in context. They also act as a natural break, as row upon row of faces can make a page appear too busy and overpowering.

A FAMILY EFFORT

Get the whole family involved when arranging and laying out the pages. Ask members to write and design labels, mount or draw colorful borders around their favorite snapshots, and note why they perceive particular images to be so special.

A child's view of the world is very different from ours. Don't discard those out-of-focus, knees-down snapshots that were the result of indulging your child or grandchild in her request to take a photograph, just like you. Instead, use them alongside the "adult" view of the same scene—for example, an adult's picture of a friend standing on the beach can contrast with the child's eye view of the friend's tanned feet in sandals. This creates a comical and touching juxtaposition and helps capture the essence of those halcyon days.

MOUNTING

Highlight images and create artistic interest by framing photographs with related mementos, such as seaweed collected from a beach or pressed flowers from a country walk. Look out for interesting-shaped items, such as shells, which can be drawn around to create attractive labels that echo significant aspects of your vacation.

Group your subjects by place, day, or theme rather than proceeding chronologically: you could have pages entitled "Children and animals" or "Things to do on a rainy day."

TIMELINE

It can be difficult when sorting through lots of family vacation photos to arrange them in chronological order. To help, create a "timeline" along the bottom edge of the page, like a tape measure with dates, so that you can write notes on memorable, funny, or disastrous events that tie in with your snapshots on the page above.

PANORAMIC SHOTS

To capture a breathtaking expanse of scenery, such as a coastline or mountain range, mount a series of photos showing aspects of the same view together. Place them side by side or overlay them, lining up the horizons as you go to create one overall shot. The resulting undulating edges of the photos will serve to add interest to the page as well as capture the expanse and grandeur of the scene.

VACATION JIGSAWS

It is fun looking through scrapbooks with kids, and it's even more fun to create some interactive elements. So why not make a jigsaw puzzle out of some of their favorite snapshots? It's simple to do. Just enlarge your chosen image on a color photocopier and mount it on a thin sheet of card cut to the same dimensions. With a soft pencil, lightly divide the image into a number of large, varying-shaped sections—just a few pieces for younger children, more for older ones. Cut out each section, then remove any remaining pencil marks with a soft eraser. Place pieces in a pretty envelope and mount them on a page of your scrapbook.

With a photo jigsaw, your children can finger favorite pictures to their hearts' content, pointing out different aspects, without your prized originals becoming marked and dog-eared. Mix a couple of vacation jigsaws together and see if your children can separate them out.

Plenty of great pictures are taken on vacation. Whether on the beach or in the country, highlight those special moments in your album.

August, 15th

Dear Zoe
I am having time on vac

Today, the beach into the water daddy for ages. It was really hot and sunny, so daddy bought me and my sister an icecream. It melted over me!
Lots of love
Amy xxx

Make sure you crop group shots carefully so you don't cut out something or someone!

club activities

A lot of us spend our leisure time participating in club or group activities. Recording these times in your family album will give you a good memento of friends made, skills learned, and ambitions achieved.

For many of us, the first club we joined was the Boy Scouts or Girl Scouts. There we learned many useful skills, such as tying knots and making campfires, and we were proud to be awarded badges for each new achievement. There is a much wider range of clubs available for children now, from chess clubs to computer clubs, judo to acting classes, stamp collecting to reading groups. There are even more activities for adults, all with some kind of goal that participants are working toward.

It's a great idea to display your photographs of these club events alongside relevant memorabilia such as badges, awards, and certificates. If the memorabilia are too large to stick on the page, add photographs of them.

CLUB ESSENTIALS

Presenting group photographs on your page is a must. This will convey the feeling of togetherness and friendship. Labeling is also essential, just in case your memory fades over the years. It's fun to attach achievements to the name, too: for instance, "John Jones: Champion Tent Pitcher of 2001."

CREATIVE CROPPING

You may find that some snapshots contain unwanted images or darkened areas. Placing a thick frame fashioned from card or paper over the photograph will not only obliterate unwanted areas but emphasize and focus the eye on the relevant subject. Overlaying your photographs in interesting juxtapositions and at slight angles will achieve the same result and also produce a feeling of

An image of your club banner and your troop number or achievement badges make ideal mementos.

Include pictures on your club page of special or memorable activities to convey the right atmosphere.

movement. Focus in on the items that were involved in your club activities, rather than just on the people who took part, to give a change of scale with close-up objects.

DECORATING THE PAGE

Make decorative borders or include motifs to highlight your hobby. You could include Boy Scout or Girl Scout badges around the edges of the page or use the club motto as a banner scrolling across the top of the display. If you are in a motorcycle club, you could reproduce some of the bikes' insignia; for a wine club,

paste in a few of the more memorable labels. Set out photos of an amateur dramatics production alongside a playbill or cast list. If you belong to a chess club, cut out silhouettes of chess pieces from colored paper.

Part of the object of this page in the scrapbook is to get across your enthusiasm for your club, so make sure the overall feel is lively and fun. Remember that people will be looking through this album in decades to come when you're not there to explain each picture, so include enough information to make clear what is going on.

TRANSFERRING IMAGES ONTO FABRIC

For a unique cover to a scrapbook dedicated to clubs or activities, attach a piece of cloth with a favorite photo transferred onto the front. It makes a great jacket, and creates a totally personalized look.

1 Photocopy your image and place it face up on a flat surface.

2 Apply a generous layer of image transfer paste (from craft stores) to

cover the surface of your photocopy.

3 Place the image face down on your fabric and cover it with a paper towel. Press firmly in place with a rolling pin. Remove the towel and leave the image to dry overnight.

4 Using a wet sponge, carefully rub away the photocopy paper to reveal the transferred image. When dry, seal with another layer of image transfer paste.

pet pals

Most pets are much-loved members of the family unit. A dog- or cat-lover may indeed find that in a year's worth of photographs there are almost as many photographs of their pet as of their children.

Include your pets' name tags next to pictures of pets that have passed away, or anything that your pet was fond of, such as a label from a can of favorite food or a snippet of a plant from the garden.

Most domestic animals have a shorter lifespan than humans, so over the years more than one pet companion will have brought joy to your life. When sorting through snapshots, take a little time to consider if you want to dedicate a single page to each particular animal or group together images using themes, such as outdoor or walking shots, or indoor relaxing pictures. You may prefer instead to build up a running commentary that illustrates the years rolling by and the different pets you've had. When mounting photos of a number of different pets on the page, you can again use these tools or create a montage of varying themes. Overlapping, tiling, or combining your images in the same manner as a collage will add impact to the page. Just remember to leave room for any data you wish to include to create a complete picture of your pet's life.

ANIMAL GALLERY

Create a portrait gallery of pets. Start with some favorite pet portraits and an elaborate paper frame for each one (you can cut the frames out of paper yourself or buy them from a good stationery or craft store). Cut the head and shoulders of your pet out of a photograph, then arrange the frame over the picture so that the shoulders fit under the lower edge of the frame, but your pet's face or nose overlays its upper edge. Your pet will appear to be looking out of the picture. Add a paper scroll below the frame with the pet's details. This makes an amusing display, especially if a hamster or rabbit is placed alongside the family dog or pony!

IN THE DOGHOUSE

Make a row of little dog kennels using colored paper, each with a flap for the kennel door. Glue a picture of your dog behind the flap and use a small loop of cord or thread and a

tiny button (fixed onto the paper or card carefully with needle and thread) to hold the flap closed.

PET PEEPSHOW

Children will love peepshows of their pets. Choose a picture taken around your garden or home that focuses on one large object, such as a tree or a sofa, behind which the pet can "hide." Take a second photo which shows your pet smaller than the item in your first image. Cut out your pet and glue a thin strip of card to the back of the cut-out so that you have a lollipop shape. Use a craft knife to cut horizontally along one edge of the large object in your first photo. The slot must be wide enough for your pet picture to pop out. Thread the strip of card behind the photo, leaving it protruding from the base of the cover picture. Glue the main photo into your scrapbook, leaving a gap for the strip at the base, but not wide enough for the picture at the top of the strip to pull through. Once fixed, you'll be able to pull or push on the strip of card to create your peepshow.

KEEPSAKES

Take a look at your pictures and think about what it is in the images that delights your pet so much—a dog playing in a pile of leaves, or a cat rolling around in a clump of catnip. Mount related ephemera, such as a pressed leaf or dried catnip, and position them alongside the photo.

PAW PRINTS

Adding a few well-placed paw prints will not only add movement to the page but will also add a welcome design element. These decorative motifs can be used to frame a group of images or arranged on the album page alongside a series of pictures of your pet running or walking.

Names of my "T" kittens:
Tilly
Terence
Tommy
Tamsin
Tara

outdoor adventures

Outdoor pursuits, such as running, mountain climbing, hang-gliding, and skiing, are among the hardest subjects to get across successfully in an album, as they tend to be fast-paced and set against a wide backdrop—but here are a few ways you can try.

Sometimes outdoor adventures will be so fast-paced and action-packed that the best photo-opportunities may be lost in a whirl of adrenalin; or if you did manage to click the shutter, the results are often disappointing. If your "action shots" leave more to the imagination than you'd intended, why not cheat a little and have some fun? Cut out a figure in a suitable sporting action pose from a brochure or sports magazine, then replace the face with a similar size face of a family member. As if by magic your father (or grandparent!) will be racing down the piste or shooting down the rapids in perfect focus. For fun with other family members, use a scene stolen from a vacation brochure and fix cut-outs of the entire family skiing down the trail or teetering on top of a snow-capped mountain.

THE GREAT OUTDOORS

Make sure your layout does justice to the landscape in which the activity takes place. If it is particularly scenic, such as snow-covered mountains or an azure ocean, you could blow up a wide-angle shot to form a backdrop to the page. Whatever you do, don't crowd the page; you want to create a feeling of immense space. One large, stunning shot could well be more effective than several smaller ones (as shown on the opposite page).

CREATE A 3D EFFECT

Action or outdoor scenes really jump into life with a 3D effect. If you have a few images of the same scene, then you can create an artistic impression of your own. Cut out the largest central subject and keep it for later. Then cut the background into small pieces (the sky, ground, mountains) and stick them into place mosaic-style on the page.

Finally, position the central subject doing the outdoor activity in the middle using a thin double-sided adhesive foam pad so that the figure appears to stand out, as a 3D image.

DECORATIVE DEVICES

Sporadically placed cut-outs of sports equipment, such as golf clubs, a football, a tennis racket, and so on, can serve as borders or, if made larger, can even be used as backgrounds to your visual display.

GET CREATIVE

A very strong image with no distracting background detail is the ideal candidate for an exploded picture. Simply photocopy and enlarge the original photograph, then cut it into equal squares and reassemble it on the page, leaving a little space between each section. This works especially well with sports pictures, since it imparts a sense of movement to the static image.

suppliers

US

CRAFT CATALOG
PO Box 1069
Reynoldsburg, OH 43068
Tel 800 777 1442
Intl tel 740 964 6210
Fax 800 955 5915
Intl fax 740 964 6212
www.craftcatalog.com
www.scrappersalley.com

DICK BLICK ART MATERIALS
PO Box 1267
Galesburg, IL 61402-1267
Tel 800 828 4548
Intl tel 309 343 6181
Fax 800 621 8293
www.dickblick.com

JERRY'S ARTARAMA
5325 Departure Drive
Raleigh, NC 27616
Tel 800 827 8478
Tel in NC 919 878 6782
Fax 919 873 9565
www.jerrysartarama.com

JO-ANN
2361 Rosecrans Avenue
Suite 360
El Segundo, CA 90245
Tel 800 525 4951
Fax 310 662 4401
www.joann.com

MICHAELS
850 North Lake Drive
Suite 500
Coppell, TX 75019
Tel 800 642 4235
www.michaels.com

PEARL
1033 E. Oakland Park Boulevard
Fort Lauderdale, FL 33334
Tel 800 221 6845
Fax 800 732 7591
www.pearlart.com

CANADA

CURRY'S ARTIST'S MATERIALS
2345 Stanfield Road, Unit 3
Mississauga, ON L4Y 3Y3
Tel 416 798 7983
Toll free 800 268 2969
Fax 877 772 0778
www.currys.com

ISLAND BLUE PRINT CO.
905 Fort Street
Victoria, BC V8V 3K3
Tel 250 385 9786
Toll free 800 661 3332
Fax 250 385 1377
www.islandblue.com

LOOMIS & TOLES ART STORES
254 St. Catherine Street East
Montreal, QC H2X 1L4
Tel 514 842 6637
Toll free 800 363 0318
Fax 514 842 1413
www.loomisandtoles.com

OMER DE SERRES
334 St. Catherine Street East
Montreal, QC H2X 1L7
Tel 514 842 6637
Toll free 800 363 0318
Fax 514 842 1413
www.omerdeserres.com

AUSTRALIA

ART STRETCHERS CO PTY LTD
PO Box 287
Brunswick Vic 3056
Tel 03 9387 9799
Fax 03 9380 4825
www.artspectrum.com.au

ECKERSLEY'S
93 York Street
Sydney, NSW 2000
Tel 02 9299 4151
Fax 02 9290 1169
www.eckersleys.com.au

index

acknowledgments

The author would like to thank Lizzie Orme for her advice on photographic techniques, red eye, and so on.

The publisher would like to thank everyone who helped by contributing their wonderful photos and other bits and pieces: Sophie Collins, James and Olivia Coulling, Viv Croot, Anna Davis, Caroline Earle, Chris French, John Grain, Joy Harnett, Ivan Hissey, Sarah Howerd, Anna Hunter-Downing, Tonwen Jones, the Lanaways, Steve Luck, Andrew Milne, Martyn Oliver, Dominic and Kate Saraceno, Tony Seddon, Michael Whitehead.